Bubbles....Up!

By **Jacqueline Davies**

Illustrated by **Sonia Sánchez**

KT KATHERINE TEGEN BOOKS
An Imprint of HarperCollins Publishers

PLUNGE!

under
under
under

Bubbles . . . UP!

mouth bubbles

nose bubbles

ear bubbles

rear bubbles

Bubbles

full of color,
full of sun
light,
light as butterflies . . .

'til   up   they   rise

And you **burst** through!

Surface like a porpoise!

shoot like a rocket ship!

zoom like a car!

You are a star!

You toss your head, water *falling*...

Mom is c-a-l-l-i-n-g...
Your hair a crazy updo. You.

You wave to Mom who watches over
young one
who does not swim,
who guards the edge,
who walks the rim.

But you—

Laugh
and
laugh

Duck—
and up!

until . . .

You under-sit.

You under-talk.

You under-smile.

You under-walk.

You sometimes sit.

You under-stand.

You under-handstand.

You.
You understand

The under world is filled with wonder
Liquid luster
Treasure to plunder

UNTIL . . .

A far-off . . .

rumble . . .

RUMBLE . . .

RUMBLE

Run for cover.
Everybody under.
Shuddering shoulders.
Huddling, colder.

The sky—a **flash!**
All eyes uplift . . . and then . . .

The rain comes

D–O–W–N–!

drenching, drowning, soaking, choking,
filling, spilling, overflowing,

so loud it makes your eardrums ring
so loud it makes the young one cling
so loud until—it slows and slows and slows

until it's over.
Done.

It's time for fun!

The all-clear sounds
And you are **IN!**

PLUNGE!

under
under
under

Bubbles . . . **UP!**

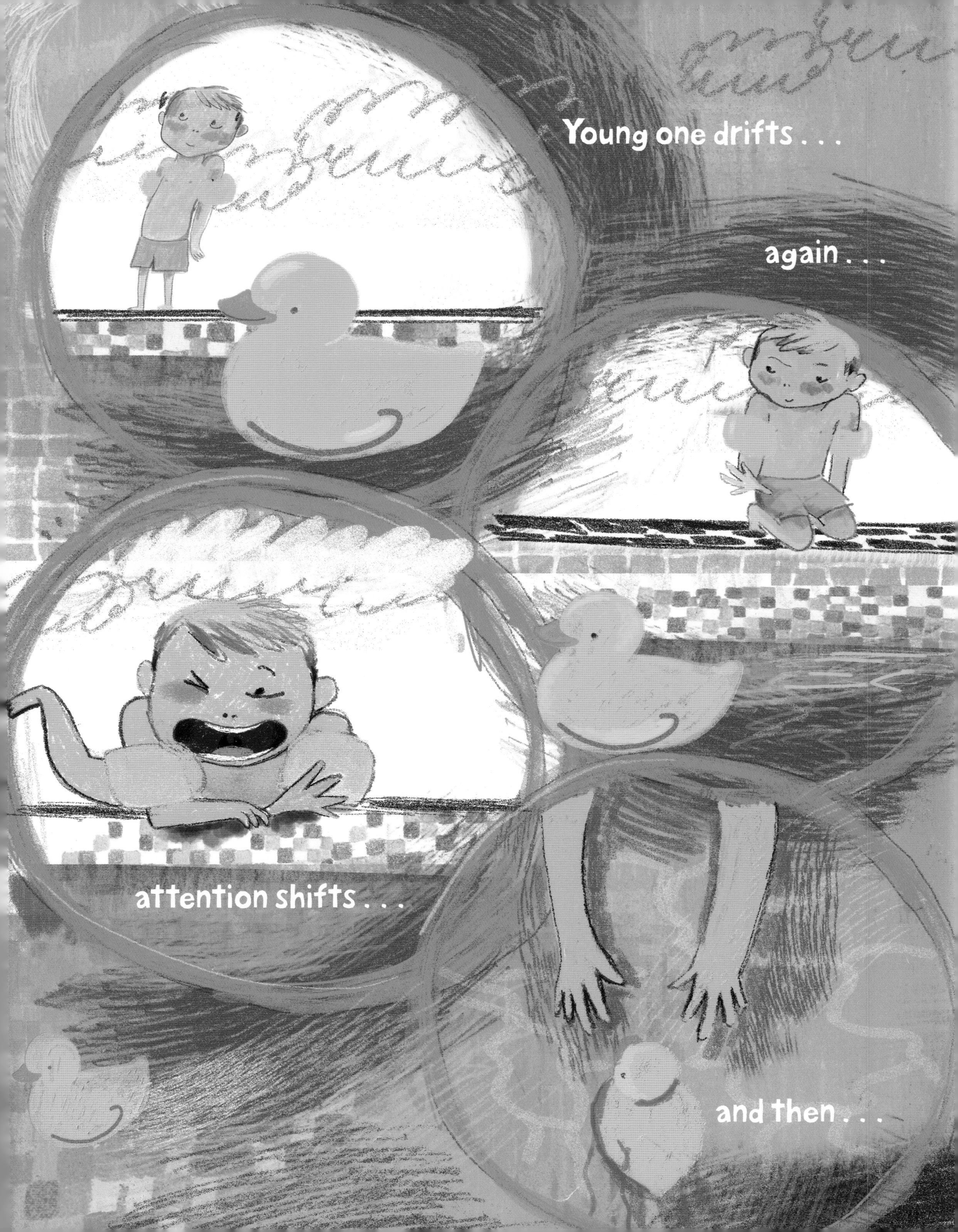
Young one drifts . . .
again . . .
attention shifts . . .
and then . . .

But you are fast and first,
    —aqueous—
A watery dolphin, all flash and fin,
You tuck your chin, dive deeper in.

PLUNGE!

Then up up **UP!**

Bursting through!

You!
You—the Superhero!

Keeping the gold
from the world down under.
Wonderful you. You are a **wonder.**

Mom hugs
    and holds
        and loves with
            big arms that wrap towels 'round

But you—*You!*—
    You have no time for mushy stuff.
    You've had enough! And so you . . .

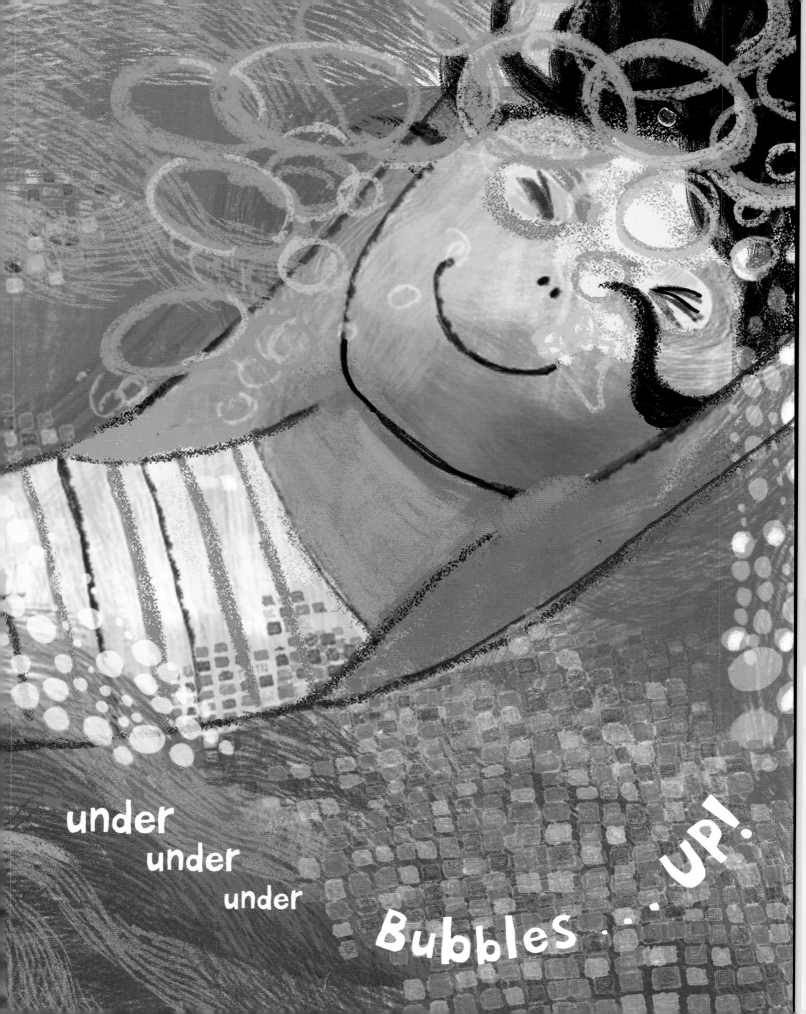

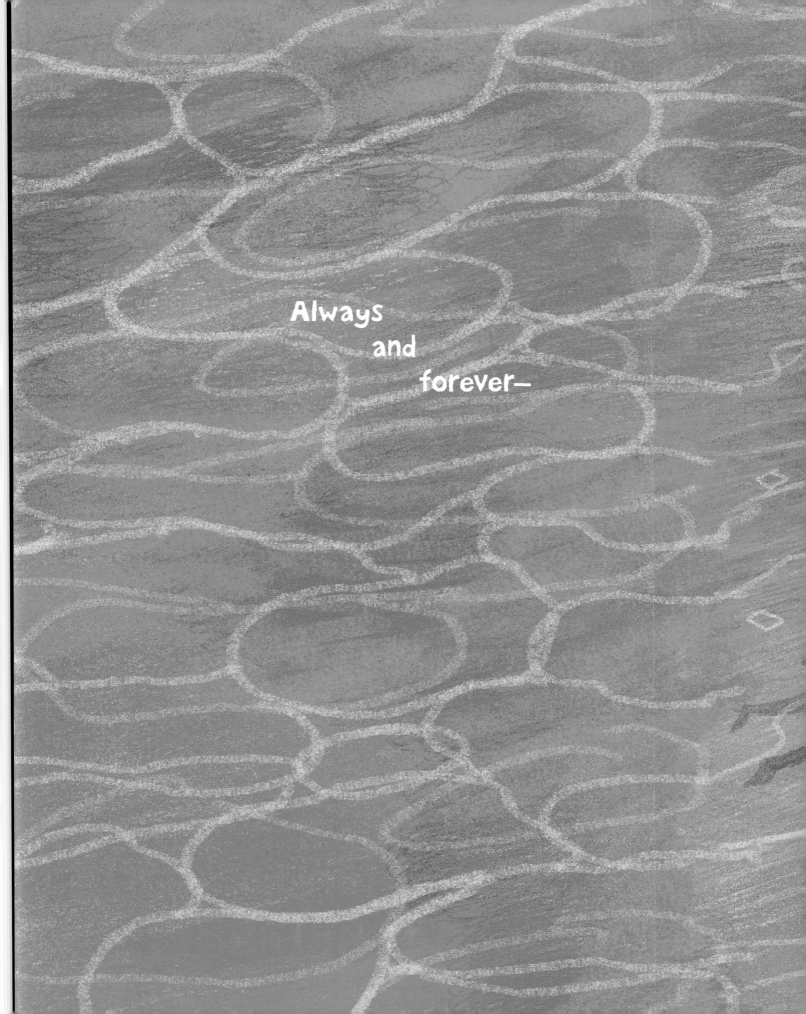

Always
and
forever—

Bubbles . . . rise . . . UP!

To Maria
—J.D.

A mi familia
—S.S.

Katherine Tegen Books is an imprint of HarperCollins Publishers.

Bubbles . . . Up!
Text copyright © 2021 by Jacqueline Davies
Illustrations copyright © 2021 by Sonia Sánchez Martínez
All rights reserved. Manufactured in Italy.

ISBN 978-0-06-283661-8

Typography by Rachel Zegar
21 22 23 24 25 RTLO 10 9 8 7 6 5 4 3 2 1
❖
First Edition